Dear Parent:
Your child's love of reading starts here!

Every child learns to read in a different way and at his or her own speed. Some go back and forth between reading levels and read favorite books again and again. Others read through each level in order. You can help your young reader improve and become more confident by encouraging his or her own interests and abilities. From books your child reads with you to the first books he or she reads alone, there are I Can Read Books for every stage of reading:

SHARED READING
Basic language, word repetition, and whimsical illustrations, ideal for sharing with your emergent reader

BEGINNING READING
Short sentences, familiar words, and simple concepts for children eager to read on their own

READING WITH HELP
Engaging stories, longer sentences, and language play for developing readers

READING ALONE
Complex plots, challenging vocabulary, and high-interest topics for the independent reader

ADVANCED READING
Short paragraphs, chapters, and exciting themes for the perfect bridge to chapter books

I Can Read Books have introduced children to the joy of reading since 1957. Featuring award-winning authors and illustrators and a fabulous cast of beloved characters, I Can Read Books set the standard for beginning readers.

A lifetime of discovery begins with the magical words **"I Can Read!"**

Visit www.icanread.com for information on enriching your child's reading experience.

For Diana, who welcomes members of every club
—H. P.

For Rose, with her feet in two puddles
—L. A.

Gouache and black pencil were used to prepare the full-color art.

I Can Read Book® is a trademark of HarperCollins Publishers.
Amelia Bedelia is a registered trademark of Peppermint Partners, LLC.

 Printed in the United States of America. For information address HarperCollins Childrens Books, a division of HarperCollins Publishers, 10 East 53rd Street, New York, NY 10022.
www.icanread.com

Library of Congress Cataloging-in-Publication Data

Parish, Herman.
Amelia Bedelia joins the club / by Herman Parish ; pictures by Lynne Avril.
pages cm.—(I can read! 1, Beginning reading)
"Greenwillow Books."
ISBN 978-0-06-222131-5 (hardback)—ISBN 978-0-06-222130-8 (pbk.) [1. Schools—Fiction. 2. Clubs—Fiction. 3. Friendship—Fiction. 4. Humorous stories.] I. Avril, Lynne, (date), illustrator. II. Title.
PZ7.P2185Aos 2014 [E]—dc23 2013031170

13 14 15 16 17 18 LP/WOR 10 9 8 7 6 5 4 3 2 1 First Edition
Greenwillow Books

by Herman Parish ✿ pictures by Lynne Avril

Greenwillow Books, *An Imprint of* HarperCollins*Publishers*

Hh

Amelia Bedelia loved her school.

She liked the way everyone got along.

They worked together.

They played together.

They took turns and shared everything.

"Let Pat have a turn."

"Daisy gets the glue next."

"You can go

ahead of me."

"I like your idea better."

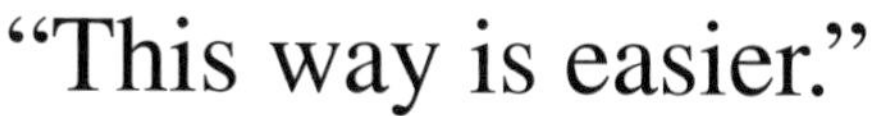

“This way is easier.”

“Try some of my chips.”

Amelia Bedelia’s class
always got along . . . until it rained.
That was when her class split in two.

"We are the Puddle Jumpers!"

"We are the Puddle Stompers!"

Puddle Jumpers took running leaps
and flew over puddles.

Puddle Stompers took running leaps and landed in puddles.

“Come sail over puddles with us,”
said Clay.
“Puddles are not big enough
to sail across,” said Amelia Bedelia.

“Come dive into puddles with us,”

said Holly.

“Puddles are too small to dive into,”

said Amelia Bedelia.

Both clubs wanted Amelia Bedelia.
Jumping and stomping looked like fun.
She liked every Jumper and Stomper.
But if she picked one club
she might hurt the feelings
of her friends in the other club.

Amelia Bedelia asked her teacher for help.

"It sounds like you are torn

between two choices," said Miss Edwards.

"You are right," said Amelia Bedelia.

"And it really hurts!"

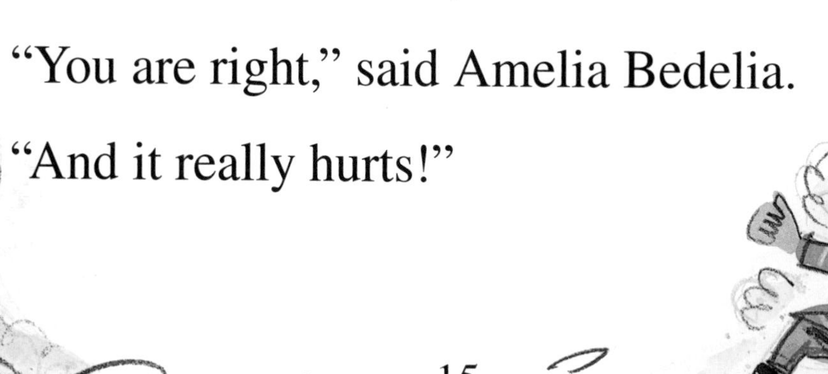

After school,

the Stompers and the Jumpers

tried to make Amelia Bedelia

choose one club or the other.

"I'll decide at recess tomorrow,"

Amelia Bedelia told them.

Amelia Bedelia's mother
was waiting for her at the bus stop.
"Rain, rain, go away.
Come again another day!"
said her mother.

"Not another day," said Amelia Bedelia.

"Rain and puddles, don't come here.

Come again another year!"

"Sorry, sweetie," said her mother.

"It is going to rain buckets tonight."

Amelia Bedelia was worried.
Buckets of rain tonight meant
millions of puddles tomorrow!

At supper, Amelia Bedelia told her parents about being caught between the two clubs.

"Wow!" said her father.

"You are in a club sandwich."

Amelia Bedelia knew her dad was joking, but at least he knew how she felt.

“Why choose?” asked her mother.

“Can’t you join two clubs?”

Amelia Bedelia stopped chewing.

That was the answer!

She hugged her mom.

At last she knew just what to do.

The next day, it stopped raining
right before recess.
The playground was filled
with oodles of puddles.

Jumpers and Stompers rushed outside.
Everyone wanted to hear which club
Amelia Bedelia was going to join.

“I am joining my own club!”

said Amelia Bedelia.

“It is called the Hop, Skip, and Jump club.”

Then she showed them what to do.

First she hopped over a puddle.

“Hooray!” said the Jumpers.

Then Amelia Bedelia skipped
to another puddle
and jumped into it with a splash.

"Yippee!" cried the Stompers.

Every one of the Jumpers and Stompers
wanted to be in the
Hop, Skip, and Jump club.
Even Miss Edwards!

“Nice work, Amelia Bedelia,”

said Miss Edwards.

“By joining your own club,

you joined the other two clubs together.”

Amelia Bedelia was not thinking about that.
She was just happy to see her class getting along again, even in the rain.